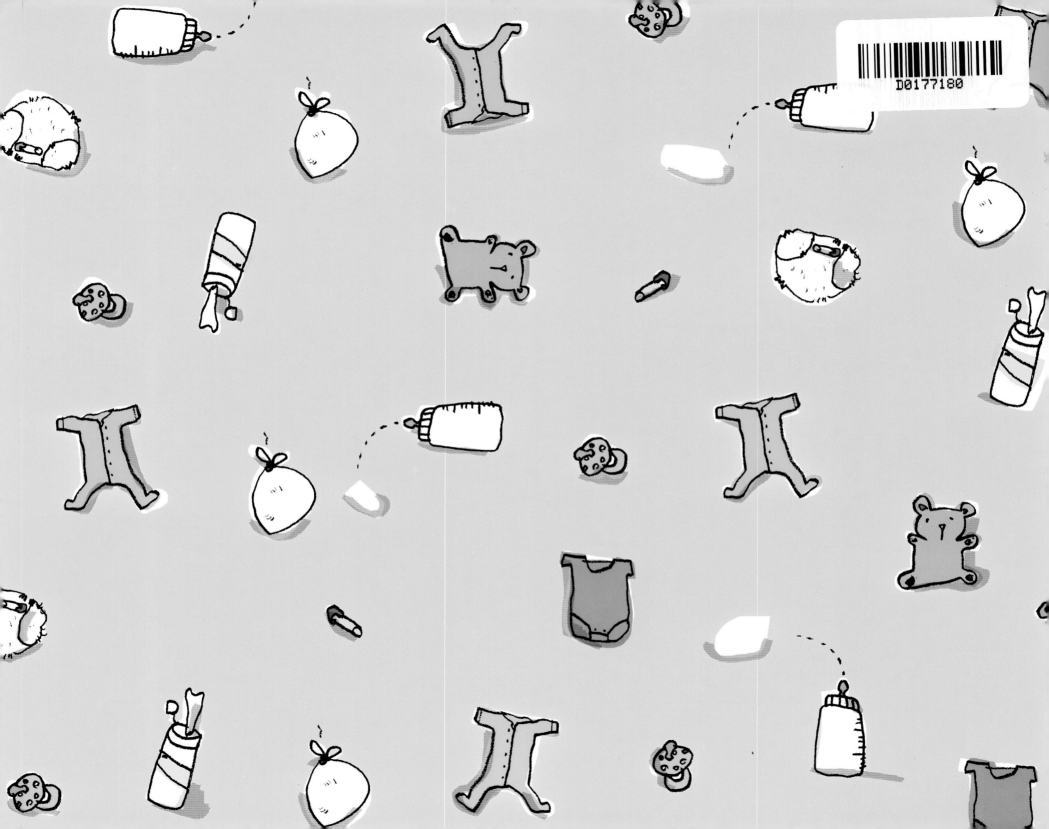

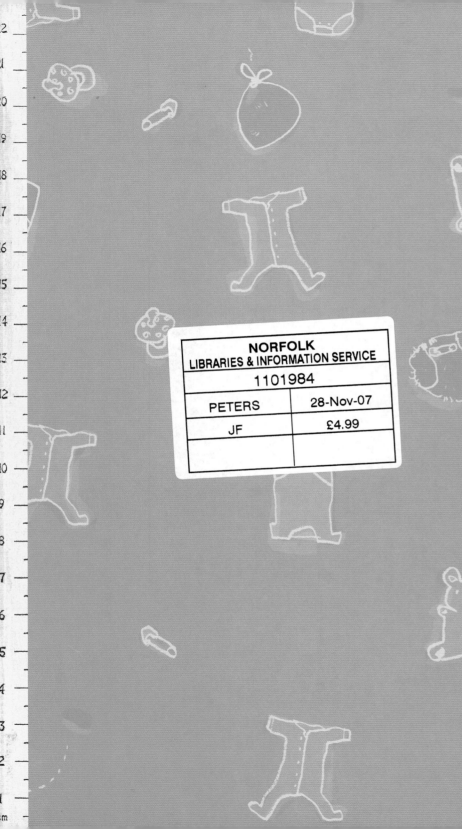

To 7lb 10oz Elsie Scarlett Gray – **K. G**
To 8lb 12oz Alfred Reed and
168lb 7oz Tim – **S.N**

BABY ON BOARD
by Kes Gray
Illustrations by Sarah Nayler.

British Library Cataloguing in Publication Data
A catalogue record of this book is available from
the British Library.
ISBN-10: 0340 878010
ISBN-13: 9780340878019

First HB edition published 2003
This PB edition published 2004
10 9 8 7 6 5 4 3

Published by Hodder Children's Books
a division of Hodder Headline Limited
338 Euston Road London NW1 3BH

Printed in Hong Kong

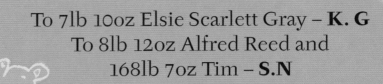

Mum's really smiley and her cheeks are all rosy. Dad says that's because she's blooming. He wants to call the baby Doug. Mum says no blooming way!

Two months:
He's half a
piece of
chewing gum
long.

He's still a blob but his arms and legs are beginning to grow. Dad wants to call him Bob.

Three months:
    He's as big as
        Mum's thumb.
    He's got eyes
        but he
            can't
                open
                    them!

I reckon it's too dark inside Mum's tum to see anything anyway. Mum keeps feeling sick in the morning. Dad says maybe we should call him Lou.

Four months: His teeny tiny fingers have tinsy winsy finger nails.

Mum has felt him wriggle.
Dad says we should call him Elvis.
Mum keeps eating pickled onions.

Five months:
He's about the size of my action doll
but nowhere near as muscly.

When I put my hand on Mum's tum I can feel him kick! Dad thinks he's going to be a footballer and that we should call him Fabio. Mum says think again.

P.S. She's buying bigger bras.

Six months: He still hasn't opened his eyes yet but he's as tall as a ruler and as heavy as Biffo's dinner.

Dad thinks we should call him Conan because he's bound to be a wrestler. Mum keeps wanting to do a wee.

Dad thinks he's going to be a really tall basketball player and that we should call him Marvin.

Boo!

P.P.S. Mum's buying bigger knickers too.

Eight months: He's as long as my arm. His brains are growing really fast and he's opened his eyes and guess what?

He's turned upside down!

Dad reckons he could have gymnast potential and that
we should call him Sergei. Mum gets cross a lot at the moment.
She needs a pillow under her bump to
help her sleep.

Nine months: He's still upside down. He looks like a real person and he's ready for launch.

Dad has packed a bag to take to the hospital. It's got Mum's medical notes in it, a towel, some nappies, boob cream, ladies things, a nightie, a hair brush, a scrunchy, three pairs of knickers, a toothbrush, some slippers, Dad's football magazine and his yoyo.

Dad says Mum should practise her breathing.
Mum says Dad should practise sleeping on the sofa.

Baby on Board

Conceived by Kes Gray
Illustrated by Sarah Nayler

h
Hodder
Children's
Books

A division of Hodder Headline Limited

Mum and Dad have
been at it again.

There's a baby growing
in Mum's tum.

NEWS
Flash

I'll keep you informed!

One month:
He's a teeny
weeny blob,
only half a
centimetre
long.

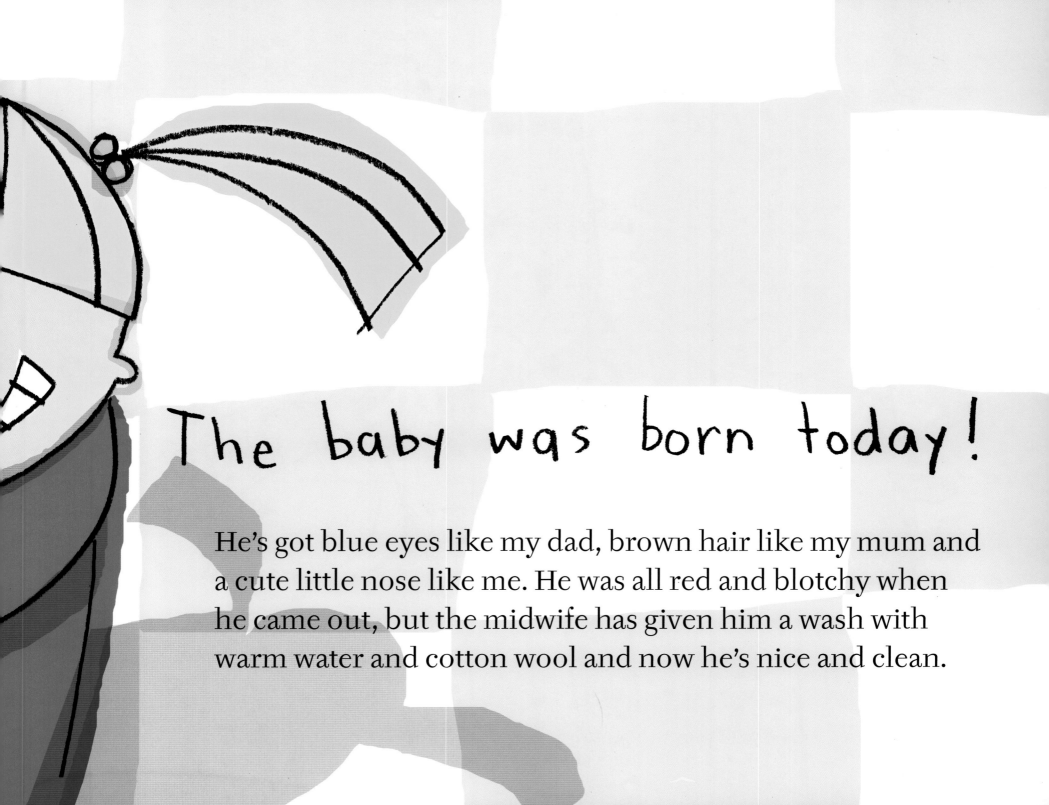

The baby was born today!

He's got blue eyes like my dad, brown hair like my mum and a cute little nose like me. He was all red and blotchy when he came out, but the midwife has given him a wash with warm water and cotton wool and now he's nice and clean.

I'm really excited.
Dad's really proud and
Mum's gone right off
pickled onions.

I think a better name
might be Susan.

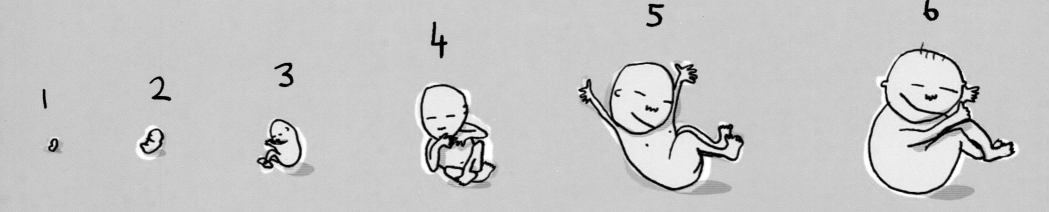